Entangled Hearts

The intricate web of love and betrayal, passion and Pain

By KJ Winchester

ENTANGLED HEARTS

First edition. May 10, 2023.

Copyright © 2023 KJ Winchester.

ISBN: 979-8223337836

Written by KJ Winchester.

Also by KJ Winchester

Entangled Hearts

Watch for more at www.theblogletters.com.

Table of Contents

The Secret

The Storm of Temptation: Clare's Dilemma

In the heart of a moonless 1859 Victorian London night, Clare Hawthorne found herself caught in the storm known as Temptation. The rain-soaked cobblestone streets mirrored her inner turmoil as she paced within the confines of her opulent Hawthorne Manor bedroom. Her fiery red hair and sapphire blue eyes exuded an untamed spirit that belied her noble upbringing.

Her heart was torn between two worlds: one that promised a life of nobility and security by becoming the wife of Phillip Chelmsford, the wealthy and formidable heir to a grand estate; the other, a passionate whirlwind romance with Jacob, a seemingly nobody whose entrancing amber eyes and tragic charm stirred something deep within her soul.

The ominous storm brewing outside was but a reflection of the tempest raging in Clare's heart; it held a deep and dark secret kept for so long from her family. A sense of foreboding filled the air as she felt compelled to decide – to conform to her family's expectations or to follow her heart into the unknown.

No matter which path she chose, both would shatter her world forever.

Beyond the wrought-iron gates of Hawthorne Manor shrouded in mist, Jacob emerged from London's cobblestone underbelly — a beacon of wisdom and charm that stood like a steadfast sentinel against societal norms. With amber eyes that illuminated even the darkest recesses of Clare's soul, he proved to be an enigmatic figure that piqued her curiosity. A former South African slave who shared her artistic predilections, Jacob abruptly altered her perception of life beyond rigid societal constructs.

Clare looked out her window. Her heart raced at the sight; it was Jacob, his rain-drenched silhouette illuminated by fleeting bursts of lightning. With desperation and yearning in their eyes, they exchanged only glances through the cascading rain.

Summoning all her strength, Clare slipped away from her opulent prison and out into the tempestuous night, embracing its chaos and uncertainty. Her noble life quickly felt like a distant dream as she felt Jacob's trembling touch; together, they stood at the precipice of truth, passion and peril.

"Jacob, my dearest love, what are we going to do? My family will never accept our union." "We will figure it out together, Clare. I love you and won't let anything come between us." Jacob replied as he embraced Clare hoping never to let her go.

As they huddled beneath a blossoming magnolia tree in defiance of propriety's watchful eye, Clare and Jacob conversed feverishly beneath shimmering constellations.

Their mutual infatuation blossomed as quickly as it did prophetically against the backdrop of Victorian distrust. Their clandestine meetings offered Clare bittersweet reprieves from the expectations bestowed upon her, allowing her to breathe in the intoxicating fragrance of freedom.

The consequences for her choice were severe — losing her family's respect, being disowned or worse — revealing secrets that could ignite another storm altogether. Yet Clare understood that some storms must be faced head-on before finding calm once again.

As Clare confronted her dilemma, she knew that regardless of the consequences, she would live by her heart's desires. Savouring each passionate kiss and whispered vow between herself and Jacob, they promised to navigate the stormy seas together, basking in the tempest of forbidden love and entangled hearts. Alas, their secret was soon to be discovered with life-changing consequences.

Six Months Earlier - Worlds Collide: Clare's Internal Battle

The sunlit morning illuminated the drawing-room window as Clare gently sipped her tea, contemplating the fragrant gardens at the Hawthorne estate. It was a picturesque scene that belied the turmoil brewing within her soul.

"Such a flawless sky," Clare remarked to her mother, who remained blissfully unaware of the impending storm enshrouding her daughter's heart. Eleanor Hawthorne sipped her tea contentedly and savoured these quiet moments in secret solitary thoughts.

As evening fell, Clare clung to her father's cherished Shakespeare anthology with tremulous hands. Surrounded by lavish décor that should have brought comfort only served to amplify her sense of entrapment.

A choice lay in this suffocating embrace of wealth and status: smother her desires or release them unto the world — an unthinkable betrayal that could shatter bonds built on generations of loyalty and trust.

Torn between obligation and forbidden passion, Clare was unwittingly drawn towards an inescapable tempest. With each moment, the brewing storm grew wilder, threatening to unleash a torrent of heartache and peril upon the lives entwined by destiny and desire.

Clare's family, apart from her mother, were staunch supporters of slavery and became discontented with the government of the day, which legislated the end of slavery in England in 1835.

"A lady must remain ever vigilant against these beasts that are slaves," warned Agnes, Clare's stern governess, with a frosty gaze. Yet when Clare met the captivating Jacob in their clandestine encounters—at safe distances from prying eyes—his eloquent stories and fiery spirit made her question everything she thought she knew about society.

Clare and Jacob whispered rebellious ideas of freedom, love, and soaring dreams in shadowy corners of forbidden gardens or under dead maple trees with cracked bark forlornly framing the stars. Shared between their passionate souls, the dangerous allure of these meetings sent shivers down their spines—both from fear and excitement.

Their meetings seared forbidden caresses into her alabaster skin, and the poems he composed in her stolen moments warmed her heart. But as their secret love blossomed, so did the risk of discovery by Clare's family, Phillip Chelmsford, and a disapproving society ready to condemn them.

Choices Amidst Shadows: A Fateful Discovery

Clare faces the tempest of her heart. Caught between the ironclad obligations of family and her fervent ardour for the enigmatic Jacob, her melancholic poet shrouded in secrets, Clare stands on the precipice of perilous desire.

Amidst clandestine rendezvous and the intoxicating danger of forbidden passions, Clare's world threatens to crumble underfoot. Her heart was violently torn asunder by the looming betrothal to Phillip Chelmsford – a union borne from duty rather than love — and the shadows closing in on her and Jacob's furtive trysts.

With each stolen kiss, their fear of discovery mounts, a tinderbox awaiting the spark that would ignite their cataclysmic downfall. When Jacob's veiled past is brought to light as that of a former slave, society's jagged talons would encircle them tighter still, threatening to separate them forever.

Will Clare surrender herself to the gilded cage forged from expectation or risk it all for an uncertain future with Jacob?

As tempestuous fate twists anew in this thrilling romance, she must confront her own heart's deepest desires — ones that may lead her life on a path most treacherous. Alas, the path on their road is now about to change. Their days will seem like perilous nights, and their worse fears will soon turn into terror.

As the ever-changing seasons whispered their secrets, an inescapable darkness loomed ahead, casting a shadow on the lives of the two doomed souls—Clare's and Jacob's lives would now change with the knowledge of the unborn life of their forbidden love child.

Under a silvery moon's embrace, within a hidden grove, the tormented lovers shivered in an anxious embrace, torn between confronting society's judging eyes and fleeing the unknown. Trusting only Margaret, a lithe and compassionate soul, Clare divulged her deepest secret, sending shivers down her confidante's spine as she weighed the disastrous outcomes.

"Harbouring this child shall unleash the scandalous tempest upon your family, yet surrendering to those treacherous abortion methods is fraught with peril.

Precious Clare, only you can weigh and balance this terrible decision—for all three fates entwined," murmured Margaret with a heavy heart, her words echoing through their trembling hearts like thunder.

Under the veil of twilight, Clare and Jacob continue to rendezvous in their secret garden — an oasis hidden from the judgmental eyes of society. Their hearts raced as desire and fear intermingled with every passionate embrace. Little did they know that an unexpected intruder would observe this moonlit dance.

Clare, the daughter of the formidable Lord Hawthorne, is beautiful and daring, chafing at the constraints of her father's expectations. Jacob was a dashing stranger who had quickly stolen her heart away. Together, they wove a clandestine web of promises and stolen moments, bound together by the mystery of their forbidden love.

The air was laced with tension as they spoke in hushed whispers, their eyes locked in a tender gaze that defied the cold reality beyond their secret haven. Suddenly, Lord Hawthorne emerged from the shadowy veil, his eyes burning with fury as he stared down at his wayward daughter and her unsuitable lover.

"You shall not tarnish our family name!" he bellowed, casting a menacing shadow over the trembling duo. Cornered like prey by his rage, Clare's chest tightened with anxiety while Jacob's mind raced to find an escape from this deadly trap they found themselves ensnared.

As they stood on shaky ground, facing Lord Hawthorne's ultimatum — to part ways forever or face dire consequences - Clare and Jacob clung to each other like wreckage amidst stormy seas. Their love had been awakened and could not be chained by worldly barriers.

In this tempest of emotion, Clare made a choice that would change her life forever: to defy her father's demands and follow the call of her heart. She knew that crossing this line would mean embracing a life clouded with secrets and danger — but what price would she pay for true love's desperate grasp?

With Jacob's warm touch fueling her courage, she decided to gamble everything for the chance to build a world where they could love without fear.

In a whirlwind of uncontrollable passion and perilous rebellion, Clare and Jacob embarked on planning a treacherous journey to traverse the life-changing terrain between them and the unyielding desire they could no longer deny.

They would defy all odds to grasp the precipice of forbidden love — together, they would dance through the fire, for their love was an unstoppable force of nature.

In the darkness of a judgmental world, where societal norms suffocated her very existence, Clare emerged from the fiery tempest with unwavering resolve. Bound by stringent conventions and the shackles of societal expectations, she sought liberation from her beloved Jacob.

Jacob weaved a captivating allure around Clare in this plan of fantasy in pursuing untamed freedom with his intense devotion to her. Millions of heartbeats resonated as one harmonious tune amid the tumultuous backdrop that engulfed them.

Together they painted an impassioned portrait of hope marred only by the unsettling cloak of doubt threatening their newfound purpose.

But first, she must return to the cage she called home; to see her mother and confidant Margaret, one of Clare's lady in waiting and confidant, one final time and gather her most treasured belongings.

Under the cover of darkness, Jacob clandestinely escorts Clare back to Hawthorne Manor with a plan to reunite at their covert rendezvous in the nearby woods in just two days' time.

As dawn stretches its tendrils across the sky, Clare awakens, unsettled from a restless slumber. She encounters her mother alone in the dining room, where she divulges her concealed alliance and love for Jacob – their fervent longing to burst forth from these shackles into a life of unbridled love far from England's grip.

To Clare's overwhelming elation, her mother not only agrees with their plans but urges haste in order to evade an ill-fated marriage with Phillip Chelmsford and withstand her father's imminent rage.

Later that day, Clare seeks comfort in Margaret's company — confiding in her lifelong friend about her impending escape from Hawthorne Manor's imprisoning walls. The joint dreams of Jacob and herself fleeing to a realm where freedom reigns supreme and forging a life wrapped in unyielding love are too powerful to ignore. Clare's unborn child must be spared this torturous existence and instead embraced by the vibrant future that she and Jacob so desperately desire.

With quivering determination etched in her heart, Clare braced herself to confront life's myriad challenges alongside Jacob.

Hand-in-hand, they determined to break free from England's stifling grasp to embrace a foreign land they christened destiny. Be it a dusty road leading to the impoverished corners of South Africa or a far-flung coast strewn with diverse encounters, Clare determined to give up all she once cherished in favour of the intoxicating passion that now defined their intense alliance.

After two torturous days and in the dizzying whirlwind of emotions, Clare found herself again entwined in Jacob's loving arms, compelled to escape the stranglehold of London's high society.

Together, they plotted their daring exit from the opulent prison that held them captive. But as fate would have it, just as they were on the verge of breaching the confines of their gilded cage, Phillip Chelmsford emerged from the shadows, his visage twisted with the seething knowledge of their forbidden love affair.

As tensions mounted and secrets unfurled like a poisonous vine, it was Jacob's haunting past as a former slave that was laid bare before Phillip's disbelieving eyes.

As love's flames began to burn brighter than reason or dignity allowed, heated quarrels erupted within shadowed corners where passion's torrid whispers danced like wildfire.

"Jacob, how can you let her risk her life?" implored Phillip as his sharp gaze flashed between Clare and the man who threatened to obliterate all he had planned for.

"She desires what is righteous and true," whispered Jacob, his voice thick with conviction. "For all that we have battled and bled for in our union of love that knows no bounds and for the love of our unborn child."

Struck by the raw revelation of Jacob's torment and weighed down by the burden of his own heartstrings, Phillip understood that his love for Clare could never measure up to the tempestuous connection between her and Jacob.

Braving the storm within him and knowing full well that his reputation would be marred within the ravenous circles of London society, he chose to relinquish Clare from their impending matrimonial bonds.

Finally unchained from societal shackles and fuelled by unwavering devotion, Clare and Jacob found a deeper level of determination to embark upon a limitless horizon far beyond London's stifling boundaries.

Entwined in each other's embrace, their plan forged a promising future—a testament to love's indomitable power to conquer even the most insurmountable barriers.

Later that day, their eyes met in the dimly lit corner of the cafe of the hidden alleyways of London, exchanging a secret language only they understood.

With every beat of her racing heart, Clare realised that plans have a way of changing, and sometimes not for the better. The possibility of betrayal loomed over them like a heavy shadow, unwilling to release its relentless grip.

As they clutched each other's hands across the table, they knew that fate had chosen a twisted path for them, filled with passion and danger.

A Father's Fury Has No Bounds

Just like the dimly lit street, illuminated only by the faint glimmer of a distant moon, a father's fury knew no bounds.

His heart races as passion and vengeance intertwine, driving him forth on a turbulent quest to defend his bloodline. Shadows danced like phantoms around him, each dark corner hiding secrets, whispers of desperation echoing through the cold air.

As he traversed the perilous alleys of betrayed trust with steely resolve, his breath brushed hot against the biting wind. Every step he took was laden with intent and purpose, for in the tender embrace of love and agony, there had manifested a storm that threatened to consume him whole.

And, like a lone figure torn from the pages of the most intense romantic thriller, his sorrowful past and unyielding desire for a false justice wove an intricate tapestry that cloaked his broken and shattered heart in a veil of fire.

His greatest weapon was not brute force but rather the depth of emotion that surged like a tempest within him—a tempest that would not be quelled until justice had kissed its bitter lips upon those who had wreaked havoc on all that he cherished.

As long as stars adorned the night sky and passions waged war in mortal hearts, a father's fury would echo through eternity, unbound and relentless—the ultimate testament to this false love's unyielding power that dwelled within Lord Hawthorne's pounding chest. Jacob's very life was in peril!

Once whispered mysteries hidden within the furtive bounds of Hawthorne Manor's woods and gardens surrendered themselves, Clare tiptoed towards the garden, cloaked by night, guided only by the moon's gentle rays.

A young woman defying convention, eager yet hesitant to embrace her passions as she navigates the boundaries of forbidden love and entangled hearts, who daringly ventures into the manor's gardens at night.

Weaving through the intricate paths, she marvelled at its haunting beauty: sculptures adorned with ivy and shadows playing peekaboo in the moonlight.

With each step towards an embrace yet again with her beloved Jacob, Clare seems now to be confronting the internal conflict tearing her apart — "Why am I thinking this way" contemplating whether to abide by society's expectations or follow her heart with Jacob.

A clandestine haven concealed Clare and Jacob's fervent passion in the shadow of towering oak trees. Embraced by the whispers of the wind, they longed to taste the forbidden fruit of liberty that had always eluded them.

Nestled in their secluded sylvan paradise, they continued plotting their great escape which promised to quench their insatiable thirst for freedom.

Fuelled by love and the thrill of danger, Jacob had meticulously orchestrated their daring plan, which danced on the edge of destiny itself.

As twilight discovered them entwined in anticipation, the distant cry of a gull announced that their time was near. Upon that fateful cargo ship sailing away from Plymouth in three weeks' time, Cape Town would become a beacon drawing them closer to unshackling their secret life.

Set against the stormy seascape, intertwining hearts would beat as one – Clare and Jacob racing towards liberation with tender fierceness unparalleled. A new life beyond borders and prejudice loomed on the horizon; only three weeks left before they could unchain themselves from clandestine love and step boldly into the unfettered embrace of eternity.

Only three weeks until freedom, Clare thought to herself as her heart raced with anticipation. In a whirlwind of romance and danger, Clare's life had become intertwined with that of her beloved Jacob, a man whose past stood in stark contrast to the aristocracy she was born into.

The looming shadow of Lord Hawthorne, Clare's father and a man of untold secrets, threatened their fragile love. Hidden beneath his polished veneer was a history marred by criminality and ruthlessness; a man who built his empire through illegal dealings in diamonds, slave trading and dark alliances that fueled the underbelly of London society.

As a sinister scheme took shape in his mind, Lord Hawthorne's fury over Clare and Jacob's forbidden dalliance drove him to seek an alliance with Stumpy—a nefarious character whose loyalties lay only with those who could afford them.

Driven by the impending nuptials between Clare and Phillip Chelmsford—a man whose father promised to strengthen Hawthorne's grip over the criminal underworld—Lord Hawthorne vowed to destroy the bond between his daughter and her true love.

Under the false guise of serenity, Clare and Jacob found themselves entwined in their secluded hideaway among the trees. Their stolen moments were fleeting yet cherished, but unbeknownst to them, Stumpy trailed behind them, a cruel agent of fate wielding a revolver.

Through the stillness of their intimate haven, the sound ripped through the air like thunder: three shots sent shivers down their spines as fear clutched their hearts. In one final act of sacrifice, Jacob hurled Clare across a small ditch for safety, shielded by fallen trees as death loomed nearby.

Two more shots echoed in the night, followed by silence as Stumpy emerged victorious over Jacob's lifeless body—their dreams of escape shattered by cold steel and merciless hands. And so began Clare's descent into a world of darkness, longing for the love that was so cruelly stolen from her.

Under the veil of darkness, Stumpy had apprehended Clare and thrust her back into the sinister domain of Hawthorne Manor. Once enveloped by its looming grasp, she found herself ensnared in a haunting rendezvous with her father, Lord Hawthorne. The spidery shadows revealed his sordid soul – Jacob, her lover, her dearest confidant, and father of her unborn child, lay victim to the malevolent schemes born from Lord Hawthorne's traitorous heart.

Clare's eyes were finally pried open to the treacherous façade of her creator, who once knitted an intricate mask of deception. But now, his attempts to protect her for the hand in marriage to the insipid Phillip Chelmsford were laid bare. Lord Hawthorne stripped Clare of any semblance of freedom — shackled to isolation, torn from her beloved friends and imprisoned away from her mother's tender gaze.

Alas, this tyranny would not end within the confines of The Manor. Her father contrived a dark plan to ship trembling Clare to Irish shores amongst ruffians and rogues. Enclosed in that faraway land, she would remain a captive as life blossomed within her womb. Only then would she emerge from that desolate chrysalis to unite with Phillip Chelmsford's cold embrace — forsaking love for slavery all for one man's twisted fantasy of loyalty.

Clare, a Life Without Jacob

The moon illuminated the dark mansion as Clare languished in her isolated chamber, her heart weighed down by unbearable grief. Taken captive by her own father, she found solace in the memory of Jacob – the passionate and secret love of her life. His untimely death at the hands of her father's conniving henchman left Clare with a void she could never fill.

Within those sombre walls, Clare carried the precious life of Jacob's unborn child, growing silently within her fragile womb. She felt the bitter sting of conspiracy as she learned of her father's merciless plan to send her to Ireland's windswept shores, where she would dwell amongst a clan of gypsies deeply rooted in London's criminal underworld.

These strangers would be her guardians as she prepared for the birth of an innocent soul that carried the blood of two star-crossed lovers. Yet, a cruel fate awaited the newborn child; torn from Clare's loving embrace, it would be destined for sale or shipment to distant lands, leaving a mother forever haunted by dreams of what could have been.

As the stormy seas churned relentlessly in anticipation, Clare found herself ensnared within a heart-pounding tale wrought with love and danger — a story that would echo through time and test the resolve of an afflicted soul fighting for both freedom and truth.

The fateful day had come – Clare, with a heart shrouded in sorrow, bid farewell to the England she once cherished and the people she held dear and cruelly unable to say goodbye to her beloved mother.

Tormented by the loss of her beloved Jacob, she braced herself for the perilous journey ahead: a laborious trek to Liverpool, an unforgiving voyage across the Irish Sea to Dublin, and finally, a road trip to the heart of Galway.

Dire tales of the tempestuous waters between Liverpool and Dublin had been seared into her memory — these treacherous seas had swallowed countless ships and claimed many lives. Yet despite the danger, Clare secretly prayed that this journey would set her free from her father's sinister grasp and lead her into the ethereal embrace of her dear Jacob.

As Clare embarked on the slow, gruelling journey from London to Liverpool, she struggled with both her fragile condition and the constant worry for her unborn child. Once in Liverpool, she found herself plunged into sordid living conditions — a far cry from the luxury she once knew. Surrounded by filth, disease, and destitution, Clare's eyes were opened to true human suffering outside her father's protected realm.

The passage from Liverpool to Dublin tested even the staunchest of souls. The vessel was packed with passengers of all classes, overcrowded and depleted of food and clean water. The relentless rough waves battered their spirits further, leaving everyone weary and broken.

Upon reaching Dublin's port, relief washed over Clare as a mysterious gypsy woman named Nan – meaning Grace – appeared to guide her on the final stretch towards Galway.

Their rickety cart, drawn by an old horse, carried them onward as Nan spoke in beautiful yet unfamiliar Gaeltacht. Though Clare could not comprehend Nan's words entirely just yet, their newfound companionship forged on.

After three gruelling days on the road in hunger and exhaustion, they arrived at their destination: the denizens of Galway, her makeshift family. These sly individuals lived on their wits, always in pursuit of a quick coin.

However, they revealed a softer side as they rallied to care for Clare and her unborn child.

Through the shared intimacy of these makeshift relationships, Clare unveiled her tale to Nan – a tale of true love with Jacob, only to have it savagely snuffed out by the cold hands of her heartless father.

As the day approached when Clare would bring new life into the world, the women vowed to safeguard both mother and child. But in time, Clare would be torn from this refuge and thrust back into the halls of Hawthorne Manor – shackled in matrimony to Phillip Chelmsford as another chapter of misery unfolded. Hopes dashed, and dreams shattered, but with a flicker of defiance burning inside her...

Jacob

In the mysterious embrace of the night, the crickets whispered sinful secrets under the melancholy moon. It was a night fraught with deception and darkness, where passion and peril became entwined like forbidden lovers at twilight.

The last we saw of Jacob, that formidable yet gentle soul, was his battered body, sprawled amid the wooded tapestry of leaves and grass — an innocent victim to the malevolent hand of Stumpy. Clare, the lovely enchantress who had been so tenderly captivated by Jacob's heart, found herself ensnared within the confines of Hawthorne Manor - fear clutching her like cold iron chains as she anticipated her unwilling voyage to Galway.

Jacob, a statuesque figure in both body and spirit, bore kindness in his eyes but carried formidable strength in his frame. His broad shoulders knew naught but toil and labour from sunup to sundown, never shrinking from even the most backbreaking tasks. Jacob's beginnings were that of enslavement, robbed of his childhood upon South African soil beneath the heavy hand of an English Lord. But there was a golden redeeming spark; Jacob was later sold, and his new master, land owner Mr James Bernard, proved compassionate at heart, ensuring health and education for those bound under his rule.

With each passing year under this merciful regime, Jacob acquired wisdom as effortlessly as he breathed — and when unfathomable freedom was bestowed upon him at 34 years young, his heart soared into new heights of hope.

Amongst that hope stirred the warm whispers of friendship in Samuel. A confidant as steadfast and true as any heart could ever dare to desire, they wove dreams like gossamer threads under starlit skies — dreaming of bountiful futures drenched in love and laughter. It was with Samuel that Jacob divulged his clandestine affection for Clare, so poignantly enchanted by her charms that he felt alive beyond even death's reach. Their secret rendezvous filled dusk with the vibrant hues of a timeless love that defied fear and claimed futures foreshadowed by agonised choices.

Always worried and protective, Samuel sensed danger looming like ominous clouds upon that fateful eve. Anxiety clutching his heart, he bravely ventured into the shadows to find his dear friend before the night devoured all hope — unveiling dark deeds enshrouded within the solemn night.

Patience gave way to a roaring fire of concern as every leaden moment whispered suspicion of impending despair. Under the haunting silver splendour of the luminous moonbeams, Samuel ventured toward their secret sanctum — navigating treacherous paths with an urgency born from unyielding devotion to his friend.

Hope and anguish coiled like serpents within him as Samuel finally breached that hidden haven where he stumbled upon a sight chiselled into his very soul. There, bathed in the ghostly light of nature's silent voyeur, lay Jacob - silent as the grave yet betrayed by shallow breaths that signalled life's tenuous grip. Amidst torrents of fear and remorse, Samuel cradled that hollow body to his heart — desperate for salvation in the darkness. But time was running out, and Samuel carried Jacob home upon an invisible gurney of prayer and love; his resilience was fuelled by a steadfast determination to change fate.

Shadowy streets provided them safe passage beyond prying eyes until they reached sanctuary at last. With urgency split between hope and fear, they summoned steadfast Alice to examine Jacob's broken form while gentle hands wove ministrations around wounds that kissed death so intimately.

Blessed fortune whispered its foretelling then: salvation dancing on the delicate balance between tragedy and triumph as hushed prophecies intertwined two hearts bound by secrets beneath forbidden skies.

And so it was that the tale continued, Jacob was alive...

Sarah Rebekah is Born

In the throes of chaos, the relentless march of time refused to yield. Clare's days in Galway had quickly stretched into six tumultuous months. During this whirlwind chapter, her heart found solace in the company of Nan and the other gypsy women, who had become her sisters in all but blood.

Though tinged with an air of danger, the men were nonetheless protective and compassionate toward Clare, fulfilling their unspoken duty.

As fate drew closer to the moment that would forever entwine their lives, every effort was made to cocoon Clare in comfort and care, to stifle the anxious beating of her heart.

She knew that the sharpened blade of her father's hatred loomed overhead, ready to sever her precious bond with her child. Yet, with courage burning bright in her eyes and a plea laced with tenderness, she implored for just one fleeting embrace upon welcoming the innocent life into the world. The sisterhood of gypsies vowed to honour her request.

All that remained now was to choose a name — a word that would etch itself like a secret code across their hearts, forever connecting them. For a boy, he would be called Daniel Jacob; Daniel – God's Judge – would be a beacon in the darkness. For a girl, Sarah Rebekah would reign; Sarah – Princess – twined together with Rebekah – to tie firmly. With each name imbued with such profound meaning, they stood as both a homage and lifeline to Clare's one abiding love: Jacob.

In the shivering embrace of twilight, Clare awoke with the restless stirrings of labour pains coursing through her like a pulsating tide. The long-awaited moment had come, one that had preoccupied her dreams and the whispers of women in the clandestine corners of the gypsy camp.

As dawn crept through the sky like tendrils of hope, Clare readied herself for the ordeal that loomed before her. Swathed in fortitude and yearning, she leaned on the watchful eyes of those women who saw her through.

As agony burned through her veins and sorrow ebbed beneath, it culminated in a triumphant burst from Clare's own shattered heart: into existence emerged Sarah Rebekah, a healthy baby girl bearing Jacob's eyes as an echo of the love that once was.

Storms of rapture swept through the camp as baby Sarah's innocent smile danced through Clare's life like a flickering flame. For what felt like an eternity and even beyond, mother and daughter embraced their euphoria — yet reality beckoned with its cold claw wrapped in fate.

Imparting tearful farewells like droplets on fragile petals, Clare trusted Sarah Rebekah to the arms of Nan and the clan she had come to call family. But as swiftly as joy washed over Clare, it retreated beneath waves of foreboding, whimpering under the weight of their now-separated paths. Hawthorne Manor awaited her return, ready to paint her days dim and hollow without her radiant African princess.

But somewhere beneath the looming shadows of distant nights, Sarah Rebekah smiled with Jacob's eyes — a cherished memory imprinted upon Clare for all eternity.

Jacob's Quest for Clare

Under the glistening moonlight in Galway, Ireland, Clare's tender smile caressed her newborn, Sarah Rebekah. Six long months of captivity had culminated in a heartbeat of innocence and beauty amidst the shadow that hung over them.

In another corner of this cold world, Jacob bore the marks of his trespasses against Lord Hawthorne - the gunshot wounds that had sent him into hiding. He was a lost soul searching for his beloved Clare, restlessly hunting for traces of her existence.

As days turned to weeks and memories clouded hope, Jacob's fiery resolve to unravel his love's fate went ablaze with impatience. It was time to gamble, to pierce the veil of Lady Hawthorne's mysterious existence — the only respite in a home fraught with dark secrets.

Navigating the constraints of this dangerous game would not be an easy feat. Every encounter could be a deadly trap. But Jacob knew that answers lay hidden behind her guarded facade — one last keyhole to unlock Clare's desperate reality.

Lady Catherine Hamilton, an illustrious figure in England's aristocracy, hosted Lady Hawthorne's fortnightly retreat into card games with close acquaintances. As twilight descended and preparations were made for Lady Hawthorne's departure from their brooding abode, opportunity danced in front of Jacob – risky and wild like flaming embers.

The horse and carriage was a vessel floating toward salvation or doom. With his heart racing like thunderous hooves on cobblestone paths, he would need to assure Lady Hawthorne of his intentions before making his move.

Margaret, Clare's trusted confidant in Hawthorne Manor's vast corridors, was Jacob's ghostly beacon in utmost darkness. Through cautious whispers passed from one sympathetic soul to another down the Manor's assembly line – Joseph to Margaret – their plot began unwinding. Only faith and uncertainty remained in the silent crevices between each step closer.

For a truth that could set them free or bind them forever, this was the price of love.

As dusk draped its silken cloak across the horizon, Jacob slinked toward the ornate carriage awaiting Lady Hawthorne. Nestled in its shadow, he entered the opposite door and concealed himself within the darkness. His fate rested on Lady Hawthorne's willingness to cooperate, an unknowable outcome that thrashed his pounding heart against his ribcage.

The moment of truth arrived: Lady Hawthorne, a vision of elegance and mystery, descended the manor's steps. As she stepped into the carriage, her piercing gaze met Jacob's. "Hello, Jacob," she spoke with an air of subdued surprise, giving him a glimmer of hope.

With urgency and gratitude lacing his words, Jacob unravelled the tale of Clare and their torrid love affair, the impending birth of their child, and his brush with death at the hands of Lord Hawthorne. Desperation clung to his voice as he implored Lady Hawthorne for any shred of information on Clare.

Without a second thought, Lady Hawthorne broke her silence. Her voice weighed down by sorrow, she divulged Clare's whereabouts — far away in Galway, Ireland – and the cruel fate ordained for her and their unborn child to be sold into slavery in a foreign land. Although uncertain of Clare's health, this revelation ignited a burning determination in Jacob.

But what came next was a revelation that sent shivers down his spine like frozen daggers — the foxtrot of deception danced by Lady Hawthorne and the man known as Edward Stokes. A ruthless criminal cloaked in shadows who had stolen her husband's identity, wealth, and Clare's birthright. Lady Hawthorne was shackled to this imposter in a sinister masquerade for twenty-four years.

The truth would bind their hearts as they wove intricate tales around one another like interlocking threads in a tapestry. With secrets laid bare and treacherous enemies lurking in every shadowy alcove, Jacob and Lady Hawthorne were thrust into a world of romance and danger, where only their cunning and loyalty could help reclaim their lives and unravel the deadly secrets enshrouding them.

In the dimly lit streets of London, where shadows danced with mystery and secrets whispered through the air, Lady Hawthorne's revelation about Clare's imminent return set hearts racing. The pulse of danger surrounding Edward Stokes' henchmen throbbed incessantly, intertwining with the urgency on Jacob's nerves.

Night after night, in a haunted embrace with the ticking clock, Jacob meticulously devised his plan to rescue his beloved Clare and their innocent baby daughter, Sarah. The creeping tendrils of Edward Stokes' desperation painted a sinister picture as if he could taste the threat of Jacob's mission drawing near.

Amidst the web of intrigue and fear, Lady Hawthorne vowed to be Jacob's lifeline, her loyalty unwavering as she braced herself to deliver crucial information for the sake of love and justice. Flame and shadow danced together within their hearts as they defied the darkness that hungered for their defeat. With every cautious step, they inched closer to reuniting a family torn apart by fate and greed.

As storm clouds rolled ominously over Liverpool and Dublin, sealing paths to tumultuous destinies, they knew that every second was a heartbeat away from triumph or tragedy. And as passions flared like blazing embers in stark contrast to the cold world surrounding them, Jacob prepared to risk everything for love, undeterred by the mortal dangers lurking at every corner.

Jacob's Rescue Mission

In the dark corners of fate's embrace, Jacob hatched his intricate, daring plan to free Sarah and Clare from the suffocating grasp of the elusive Irish gypsy clan in Galway. The operation was one of grand proportions, demanding people in diversely scattered locations, modes of transportation swift as the wind, a sailing vessel for silent escape through the turbulent sea, and a fortune amassed to buy hushed whispers and uncharted havens.

As we delve into the past by seven years, a piece of history found its way into Jacob's life. James Bernard, his former slave master, wore a mask of benevolence that hid his cold eyes from the world. Fortune smiled upon him, worth 50 million pounds in cash and land stretched for miles. When death finally knocked on his door, he looked back at his ten slaves and laid before them an unexpected gift — an equal division of wealth and estate they could only dream of.

Tradition dictated that once unshackled from their chains, former slaves took upon new names to mark their spirits free. For Jacob, it was out of respect and honour for the man who carved out his path to affluence that he adopted his late master's surname, Bernard. Now called Jacob Bernard, he held a treasure trove worth 5 million pounds in cash as well as land sprawling across South Africa and England like golden threads woven into destiny.

Wisdom led him as he invested without a word about his riches. When it mattered most, he knew his capacity to finance the risky mission to save Sarah and Clare. Failure was not an option.

He assembled skilled teams for each rescue: Samuel, Daniel Soy, and Caroline Beech for Sarah; Tobias Chubb, Boriston Kidd, and Mary

Tunstall by his side for Clare. Hearts pounding with urgency sang a symphony against a fate that dared to challenge them. The fire in their souls burned with the need for haste and the sharp blade of surprise as their allies.

The plan unfolded: A simultaneous rescue - Clare snatched from her captors en route to Dublin, and Sarah spirited away in Galway. Their journey would lead them all to a meeting point in Ballina, and from there onwards, and they would sail to the Isle of Islay in Scotland for safety.

Their footsteps echoed like whispers on restless soil as they followed destiny's trail. Dangers lurked around every corner, but justice remained in their hearts — a compass guiding them to victory. In love's name, they would save those who called out from the shadows, intertwined by the threads of romance in a dance with a fate that entwined them all.

The Rescue Plan

Under the veil of an ink-black sky, our fearless quartet, Jacob, Tobias Chubb, Boriston Kidd, and the enchanting Mary Tunstall, shall embark upon an odyssey of high intrigue and veiled peril. Their steadfast resolve shall carry them to the quaint village of Fishguard in Wales and onward by steam-powered vessel to the enchanting shores of Rosslare Harbour, Ireland.

A clandestine rendezvous with a figure cloaked in shadows shall usher them forward, providing loyal steeds for their treacherous journey. Racing against time itself through the verdant landscapes of Carlow and Portlaoise, they shall arrive in the moonlit embrace of Athlone. The task ahead is daunting; they must reach their destination betwixt the twilight hours of three and four in the morning.

At the heart of this tempestuous tale lies the vulnerable Clare; she would be held captive within Sean's Bar overnight—a den of treachery and deceit. Our quartet will spring their daring plan into action there, aided by secretive allies, at precisely half-past four in the morning. The unsuspecting captors' spirits were subdued by intoxicating free-flowing ale bestowed unto them by a duplicitous landlord.

In the midst of this frenzied maelstrom, our valiant party shall spirit Clare away like a fleeting shadow. Swiftly replacing their worn steeds for fresh ones in Rosscommon, Ballyhaunis, and Charlestown as they journey westward into the crimson-streaked sunset. Each determined beat of their horses' hooves brought Clare closer to liberty's embrace in Ballina.

Meanwhile, to deceive and create a diversion, Samuel, Daniel Soy and Caroline Beech will secure Sarah's freedom from gypsy hands like an intricate tapestry staining their honour with every stitch.

As darkness falls once more upon our heroes, they will join forces with the rescue team from Galway in Ballina, and as the hand of fate tickles the very cogs of destiny, a humble sea vessel shall carry them to the coastal tranquillity of Port Ellen on Islay. And only there, ensconced in nature's sanctuary, shall they find solace and liberation from the nefarious grasp of their past, in patience waiting for brighter days to return to London.

Through victory and heart-pounding daring, a story-fit crescendo swells around those determined that justice shall prevail against all odds.

Clare, Sarah and Jacob Reunited

A Reunion Like No Other

In the mysterious glow of the moonlight, shadows danced gracefully upon the cobblestone streets, enveloping the town of Athlone in an enchanting aura. Clare's heart pounded with an unknown eagerness that swelled within her chest as she arrived in this mysterious place. Unbeknownst to her, she was on the brink of reuniting with her long-lost love, Jacob – a love that burned with an intensity that could rival the fires of passion itself. Their connection ran deep, embodied in the form of their daughter, Sarah – a living testament to their unbreakable bond.

Jacob found himself at the centre of a daring rescue mission. He worked to quell the tempestuous emotions welling up inside him and waited on the outskirts of Athlone so as not to distract from the perilous task. The sands in the hourglass continued to cascade downward, allowing them to press forward swiftly and clandestinely throughout the perilous rescue.

As they neared their destination, short and anxious breaths filled the chilled air, amplifying tension and suspense as thick as fog. With every step closer to Clare's whereabouts, she unknowingly readied her soul for an event that would forever change her life. Following directions from a bribed insider, Jacob's dedicated rescue team infiltrated the Inn where Clare was held, hostage.

Clare and her fellow captor, but now friend, Nan, had been unable to find solace in sleep while their captors succumbed to heavy slumber from excessive drinking. They were completely oblivious to Jacob and his crew's imperceptibly stealthy movements through the dim innards of their hideout.

Each member of Jacob's team moved like stringless marionettes bathed in darkness, drawing ever nearer their goal. As they approached Clare and Nan's chamber, they positioned themselves strategically amidst shadows to set up their tactical surprise attack. Through synchronicity born of rigorous training, they breached the room with an unwavering sense of purpose, quickly subduing Clare's stupefied captors.

In moments, the captors found themselves confused, their minds clouded by intoxication, and were easily subdued and bound by Jacob's experienced crew. With little time to spare before the remaining enemies discovered their missing comrades, the team gathered up Clare and Nan before making a hasty retreat from the sordid confines of the once-imprisoned abode.

Moving with unrivalled agility and finesse, Jacob's crew left the town behind in a blur, knowing that a hurricane of chaos would soon follow. However, their expertise in stealth gave them an edge over any pursuers who might interrupt their escape. With their quarry safely in hand and luck on their side, the window to salvation lay open before them.

Jacob stood at a prearranged location far from danger's reach on the edge of Athlone. As the rescuing steeds approached him, he stood with open arms and tear-streaked cheeks. His body seemed to emanate radiant rays of hope that pierced through even the thickest nightfall. Clare's utmost joy was inexpressible at seeing Jacob. He is alive. Clare and Jacob, at long last, came together as if guided by destiny itself.

As they wrapped themselves around one another like intertwined vines sealing their reunion with sweet kisses amid the pressing darkness, love now transcended time itself. Every touch became an infusion of love between two souls deeply entwined in one another's essence — an ethereal connection only present in ancient mythical tales.

Yet reality cried for haste; this reunion must concede to urgency. Clare surrendered herself to Jacob's strong arms as he lifted her onto her noble steed. The rescue was complete, and now destiny had turned its gaze upon Sarah.

With unyielding determination, they charged forward on a relentless path to Ballina. The churning seas awaited their arrival, where they hoped to reunite with young Sarah. Every moment apart tore at their souls like sharp talons, yet faith was the anchor that steadied them.

Upon reaching the clandestine shores of Ballina, unease clawed at their nerves like icy tendrils. With bated breath, they saw salvation approach — a horse and carriage barrelled toward them with precious cargo aboard.

Tears of overwhelming joy flooded Clare's eyes as she raced towards the approaching vehicle. Embraced in her loving arms once more, Sarah's presence filled a void that had tortured her spirit for far too long. Clare turned to her beloved Jacob and whispered, "My dearest Jacob, your dream, your daughter, Sarah Rebekah."

With hearts intertwined, the reunited family embarked upon the vessel that would sail them through the edge of the Atlantic Ocean and onto Scotland's shores — a voyage to freedom and new beginnings. Amidst the unyielding waves, they stood strong; love had brought them back together, and love would see them triumph against all odds.

The Sins of the Father

Under the moonlit sky, in the hauntingly captivating Hawthorne Manor, a tale of deception and desire unfolded as a rose slowly revealed its hidden secrets. The man known as Lord Hawthorne, a creature of intrigue and power, concealed his true nature behind a façade of gentility and wealth. Tales of his vast estates in England and South Africa seemed to command respect from those who crossed his path, little suspecting the sinister truth — that he was none other than Edward Stokes, a man who had built his entire life on falsehood.

As he paced through the opulent halls of his ill-gained home, a passionate fire burned within him; he would do anything to protect what was now his. Though he bore the title and privileges of Lord Hawthorne, it was not enough to quench his ravenous thirst for dominance — there remained one key aspect of his deception: Eleanor, the woman who had once shared her life completely with the actual Lord Hawthorne.

Bound by an unbreakable spider's web of deceit, poor Eleanor had little choice but to conform to the wishes of this formidable imposter. Plagued by fear that her loving husband might be assassinated should she refuse, she acquiesced to share her bed with this malevolent stranger. The product of their union was an enigmatic girl named Clare, oblivious to the fact that her very existence was born from shadows.

All the while, far away in South Africa and stripped of all possessions and dignity, a destitute Thomas Hawthorne was imprisoned by Edward Stokes these past 24 years. This scoundrel had orchestrated events from behind an impenetrable veil to usurp Lord Hawthorne's aristocratic life and claim him as kin. As each day passed in sheer torment for the faithful Lord at one end of the globe and illicit pleasure for the pretender at another, destiny lay patiently in wait — for sooner or later, the web of lies would finally begin to unravel.

In the shadow of deception, Lady Hawthorne's existence teetered precariously on a knife's edge. The sinister truth about Edward Stokes' treachery left her tormented and Eleanor Hawthorne imprisoned within a world of sorrow, their fates entwined in a terrifying dance.

Day and night, fear stalked Eleanor like a ravenous beast, her destiny unknown on this heart-wrenching journey in the merciless hands of treachery. Meanwhile, Edward Stokes' malicious intentions brewed, creating a perilous event that could seal her doom.

Amidst looming threats that choked her very breath, Lady Hawthorne received an invitation to attend a ladies' conference hosted by Lord and Lady Ripley in Surrey. On that long and lonesome journey through desolate roads and hidden dangers, a fatal trap awaited — staged as an ill-fated robbery gone awry. Under the vile command of Stumpy, miscreants would base their scheme upon wicked deception and ruthless gunfire.

Haunted by peril, Lady Hawthorne placed her faith in Jacob – her last flickering light of hope. Yet her knowledge of his whereabouts remained shrouded in darkness, while unbeknownst to her, he had rescued Clare and Sarah from the clutches of evil and was now in Scotland.

Desperation took hold of Lady Hawthorne as she clung to the chance that Jacob's friends might break through the silence to send word of her plight. Thus she tasked Margaret with delivering a clandestine note to Samuel – knowing only that he was close to Jacob.

With time running out like sand through an hourglass, Margaret made haste to Samuel, whose heart filled with concern upon reading Lady Hawthorne's words. Compelled by urgency, he transmitted this vital message using the electric telegraph system — a conduit to Jacob that would secure or shatter their hope.

Three days later, under a shroud of despair, Jacob found himself clutching the parchment that bore the grave news about Lady Hawthorne. His heart raced, and anguish gnawed at his soul as he faced the harrowing task of confiding in Clare. The weight of truth crushed him, for he must reveal his knowledge of Edward Stokes, the deceptive ruse played over their heads for 24 years, and the sordid chains imprisoning her mother's life — the secret of the real Lord Hawthorne.

With each thunderous beat of his heart vibrating through his veins, Jacob feverishly penned a missive, alerting Samuel to his impending return to London that very day. He implored Samuel to gather their trusted allies, for they must urgently convene and devise cunning strategies to rescue Lady Hawthorne from her all-consuming plight.

Amidst the swirling whirlpool of uncertainties threatening to consume him whole, Jacob remained ignorant of Edward Stokes' machinations — if such plans even existed. Yet one truth pounded relentlessly in his mind: the sands of time slipping cruelly through their fingers as Edward Stokes' desperation swelled like a tempestuous ocean wave, spurred on by the dramatic rescue of Clare and her innocent child. Fueled by unyielding determination and haunted by despair, Jacob embarked on a treacherous journey — a race against fate itself — for love and redemption.

In the murky shadows of London, a tale of desperation and intrigue unfolded as Jacob tirelessly pieced together the sordid puzzle of Edward Stokes' deceit. Kindred spirits from across the city united in their pursuit of good, brought whispers of a long-forgotten rebellion to Jacob's ears. It seemed fate had intertwined their destinies with Joseph Adams, an ailing man hiding a cache of secrets as dark as night.

Jacob's heart raced with determination as, in secret, he shared his harrowing mission with Lady Hawthorne, their bond forged by a shared sorrow and fleeting moments of joy at the news of Clare and Sarah's freedom. Her eyes glistened with tears as she spoke of her connection to the enigmatic Joseph Adams, each word revealing another piece in the grand puzzle. The mystery thickened, and urgency enveloped them like a cloak.

As tendrils of curiosity and influence spread far beyond the city limits, Jacob's loyal companions ventured into the squalor of Manchester's underbelly, leaving no stone unturned in their search for Adams. Amidst decrepit streets and shadowy corners, they discovered the frail man languishing in a lonely sanitarium, ravaged by illness and remorse.

The piercing truth cascaded from his trembling lips like shattered glass, painting a vivid portrait of misdeeds and vile intent enacted by Edward Stokes. Samuel's resolve hardened like steel as Joseph Adams uttered his dying plea for justice. They would see Edward Stokes pay for his sins.

Beneath London's rain-soaked skies, Samuel returned to Jacob with grim news clutched to his chest. Together, they enlisted the aid of Scotland Yard's finest to cut through layers upon layers of deceit festering within their city's heart. Time was an enemy in this race for redemption but no match for their unyielding tenacity.

In a whirlwind of action and retribution, Edward Stokes' final reckoning arrived amidst frantic breaths and papers flying like storm-tossed leaves. As the villain was wrenched from his opulent lair, a mixture of elation and weariness enveloped Lady Hawthorne.

But their tale was far from over, for one elusive question remained: what fate had befallen Lord Hawthorne? And as the shadows of the past continued to haunt them, they knew their tormented hearts could not rest until the truth was laid bare before them. Where is Lord Hawthorne?

Clare and Sarah Return to England

As the year 1860 unfolded, the malicious Edward Stokes found himself in the cold grasp of justice, his dark deeds no longer a secret. Charges of attempted murder, the devious imprisonment of Lady Hawthorne by weaving webs of mystifying tales about her beloved husband, and a litany of harrowing assault allegations ensured that this wretched soul would be confined forever to a cell's unforgiving shadows.

In the wake of these tribulations, Lady Hawthorne bravely sought to reclaim her life from the shambles left behind. Gradually regaining her lost influence over her ancestral lands, riches, and ventures sprawled across the far-reaching corners of England and South Africa, she nevertheless cannot cease grieving for her absent husband. Her heart's poignant yearning remains unsatiated, echoing with questions and uncertainty.

And yet hope stirs in the distance — a glimmering beacon within an ocean of despair. Soon Clare shall return bearing news that warms Lady Hawthorne's injured heart: her cherished grandchild Sarah is coming home. Anticipation and joy intertwine as preparations commence, transforming the Manor into a true family haven once more.

In this swirling vortex where desperation battles euphoria, love may emerge victorious to heal wounds long carried; but mysteries still linger in every corner — can happiness become a lasting reality for Lady Hawthorne?

The day had come, shrouded in an air of mystique and anticipation; Clare would be reunited with her roots — the family home and bringing Sarah with her. Alongside Jacob, they would bring newfound hope to the once desolate halls of Hawthorne Manor.

Lady Hawthorne's heart swelled as emotions threatened to consume her; joy blended with unbridled relief that Clare was finally free from Edward Stokes' iron grip. A tide of fervour washed over her as she awaited long-lost reunions.

No more waiting, no more desperation; the future had arrived on a majestic carriage, gently treading its way up the driveway lined with well-wishers and staff from every station, united in welcoming Clare and Sarah home.

Lady Hawthorne, her heart racing to match the rhythm of the nearing hooves, was perched on the Manor's steps like a regal queen. The excitement clawed at her chest as she steadied herself for what would come. The carriage came to a halt, opening like a blossoming rose in spring; first, Jacob emerged, his arms becoming a haven wrapped around Lady Hawthorne.

As Jacob offered his hand within the confinement of the wooden vessel, Clare's delicate fingers found their way into his grasp. Time stopped for an eternity — two souls intertwining through their grip. As she emerged from the darkness of her past encased in the carriage and stepped into the sunlight that danced upon her, a vision of rebirth manifested before them. Clare had returned.

No longer able to hold back her motherly instincts, Lady Hawthorne lunged forward towards her precious Clare, cocooning her daughter in an embrace so tight it threatened to cut off circulation. Their joy radiated outward as thunderous cheers poured from all who basked in its warmth.

Momentarily stepping back, Jacob summoned Margaret, who cradled young Sarah. Gently lifting her from Margaret's arms, the infant's love lit up his face like embers sparkling in a passionate blaze. Nestled in Lady Hawthorne's waiting arms, Sarah became the newest chapter of life's miracle sewn into the tapestry of the family.

A radiant arc of hope draped itself over Hawthorne Manor, and the bonds of broken family ties intertwined once more. Grateful to have found solace within those walls, Jacob's soul swelled with pride as he breathed, declaring with a fire that could only be divine destiny; he boldly pronounces a purpose: "Let's go get Lord Hawthorne."

Lady Eleanor Hawthorne

In the lush gardens of West Sussex, a tale of passion and intrigue was set in motion. Eleanor Victoria Laidley, a young woman of refined taste and intellect, caught sight of the enigmatic Thomas Hawthorne at a picturesque garden party in April 1831. The air was palpable, with both budding romance and a sense of impending suspense.

Though Thomas was older by five years, the two quickly formed an unspoken bond that transcended social norms. Eleanor, her heart pounding with each gaze exchanged from across the manicured lawns, found herself drawn to Thomas like a moth to a flame. This mysterious gentleman—handsome, well-travelled—seemed to possess a certain magnetism that left her utterly captivated.

Risking their reputation and standing within polite society, their love blossomed in the shadows of candlelit parlours and moonlit walks. Thomas confided in Eleanor about his budding trading empire and his dreams of one day conquering the wilds of South Africa. Conversations stretched late into the night as they found solace in each other's company.

As their passion grew bolder, whispers about their clandestine courtship began to circle. The tension between propriety and desire threatened to tear them apart like a rose's petals caught in a storm. With time running out, Thomas knew he must act quickly to secure his beloved's hand before their story became a fleeting memory of stolen glances and forbidden affection.

Under the weight of expectations by society, realising their unwavering love could not be contained any longer; he orchestrated a daring plan to unite them forever: proposing marriage before Eleanor's apprehensive parents.

The stage was set for an unforgettable climax—their fate hanging precariously in the balance—as Thomas gazed into Lord and Lady Laidley's eyes and expressed his undying devotion to their daughter with words laced with emotion.

A beat hung heavy in the air until, at last, the Lord and Lady approved for Eleanor to become his wife, sealing a bond forged by love, intrigue, and passion—an eternal fire that would burn brighter with each other day they spent together.

January 31ˢᵗ 1832

"My dearest Eleanor, on this splendid day, the heavens themselves have conspired to celebrate your birth, a momentous occasion that brought you into this world, and with every passing year, you have grown more radiant and enchanting. Your presence has illuminated the darkest corners of my heart with the warmth of your smile and the sweetness of your laughter.

As I stand before you beneath the starlit night, bearing witness to the incomparable beauty of your soul, I am reminded of how truly grateful I am for every moment we have shared. Our paths have intertwined seamlessly, creating intricate tapestries that tell tales of our unending love, which have drawn me deeper into this magnetic wonder.

Eleanor Laidley, my guiding light and true north, today serves as a celebration of our love and an unforgettable embark on untold dreams. While words fail to express the exquisite nature of the emotions coursing through my very soul, it is with a heart filled with unreserved adoration that I ask you to fulfil my greatest desire: to spend eternity by your side.

Allow me to take your delicate hand in mine as I lovingly inquire: will you make me the happiest man alive by accepting my hand in marriage? Let us embark on this endless journey together. Each day with you in my life will be a brilliant masterpiece painted by our joined hearts' aspirations".

Under the starlit night, shadows danced across Eleanor's anxious face as she stood before Thomas, her heart pounding like the rhythm of an untamed tempest. The air was thick with anticipation, and secrets veiled behind their eyes.

Thomas' piercing gaze locked onto her, his azure eyes carrying the weight of their shared stories—their journey as if it played out between them like a vivid dream.

A hushed silence fell between them. Eleanor, trembling with the culmination of her innermost feelings, let her words escape, gently yet firmly: "Thomas... my heart has been wavering in this treacherous labyrinth of emotions—fear, desire, compassion—through every twist and turn that fate has thrown our way."

She paused, taking a breath that steadied her quivering soul. "But here and now, we stand once more at the precipice, daring to leap into the unknown that is love." Her voice wavered as tears glimmered in her eyes. "I confess before you...I accept your hand in marriage."

Thomas' heart pounded recklessly against his chest as he listened to Eleanor's passionate declaration. He felt the warmth of both hope and relief ignite within him as she made her choice, and silently he cherished this significant moment.

The shadows seemed to frolic with joy as the starlight flickered around them. And in that fleeting moment of light and warmth shared between two lovers destined to unite, time stood still—an eternity encapsulated within a single heartbeat.

Eleanor stepped towards Thomas, who held his arms open wide; together, they embraced their newfound promise—a bond forged in love and emotion that would shatter all boundaries and conquer every dark storm on their path.

It was an acceptance they both needed, a cleansing echo of love that reignited their souls — fastening them together for lifetimes to come. As one chapter closed on their story, the pen of destiny dipped gently into the ink to write their future — a story that would forever blur the lines between passion and fear, juxtaposing love against vehement odds.

Where, oh, Where Has Thomas Hawthorne Gone?

Enshrouded by mysteries of the night, our beacon of truth finds himself torn from the embrace of love and homeland. He faces a life of crushing solitude, relegated to the obsidian depths of a South African prison.

As he languishes, tormented by despair, vile scoundrels bask in the cruel delights of ill-gotten fortunes and hedonistic pleasures. Thomas's beloved wife, bereft and forlorn, falls prey to these wicked beings who desecrate her honour and dignity.

In this tale of heartache and sacrifice, burning rage intermingles with tender love, ardent passion battles icy dread, and fervent emotion stirs the depths of human resilience.

Where oh where is Thomas Hawthorne? Will fate ever reunite him with his cherished sanctuary?

In the depths of the South African Mountains, shrouded in mystique and veiled in shadow, there lies a man whose story is etched into the hearts of local villagers. A prisoner in his own barren, desolate world, he is shackled to his abode by the unending torment of solitude and despair.

Once a thriving pillar of affluence and joy, his life now hangs in tatters, with only memories of a prosperous past to cling onto. Ravaged by fate's cruel hand, he has been betrayed by a friend's fickle embrace and abandoned by those he cherished. His heart echoes with the cacophony of emotions — compassion, sadness, anger — drowning out what little hope remains.

Within his crumbled sanctuary amongst the mountains' embrace, time plays a cruel trick upon his weary soul. No longer a youthful sprite who danced through life with vigour and passion, his hunched figure now resembles that of an aged spectre twice his years.

Yet through the anguish and harrowing depths of his soul, there lies a prevailing ember within him that refuses to be extinguished: the eternal flame of love. As he dwells in seclusion, coping with this tapestry woven from threads of sorrow and heartache, perhaps fate may grant him one final chance at redemption, an unexpected ray of hope amidst his darkened existence.

Herein lies a tale destined to echo through the South African Mountains for generations to come — a solemn reminder that love's flickering light may still prevail even in life's darkest corners.

Twenty-Four Years Earlier

Under the embracing warmth of the South African sun in 1835, Thomas Hawthorne and his enchanting wife, Eleanor, revelled in the affluence born from their thriving enterprise. Encompassed by bountiful farmland, tender zephyrs whispered tales of joy and prosperity, mirroring the couple's unwavering affection and their determination to see their labourers flourish.

As they sauntered amidst the fields, hands lovingly entwined, the sun painted ethereal silhouettes upon their visages. Their melodic laughter harmonised with the symphony of contented workers as beads of sweat gleamed on furrowed brows — all savouring the profound bond that sprung from plights endured together. However, all was not meant to remain idyllic; a sinister cloud loomed in the wake of paradise.

With beauty as poignant as her devotion, Eleanor would trail her beloved from South Africa's sweeping plains to Sussex's stately homes. Edward Stokes, a calculating and zealous Englishman, seized control over every facet of their burgeoning business in her absence.

A riddle clothed in bespoke tailoring, Edward's cerulean gaze held secrets unfathomably. His dulcet voice commanded awe while veiling envy smouldered beneath his outward composure.

"This empire you've raised is truly extraordinary," he'd often muse in quiet moments with Thomas. Yet behind closed doors, he contemplated how to ensnare such opulence for himself.

Edward devised a sinister scheme to overthrow his unwitting benefactor as darkness consumed him. Amassing a cohort of unfaithful lackeys with twisted grins and even more twisted hearts, he planned to assail where it would wound most.

In twilight's embrace one afternoon in Queenstown plantation — foreshadowing calamity – Edward met his accomplices, wicked souls filled with rancour at Thomas Hawthorne's accomplishments.

"And so it was decreed," Edward intoned venomously, delicate fingers tracing the designs sprawled before him. "These spoils will soon be ours, and he shall know destitution."

Silence echoed his words — anticipation thrumming through the shadowy chamber.

Thomas and Eleanor basked in their Elysium, oblivious to the treacherous darkness that stained their haven. They delighted in a leisurely meal as a tempestuous storm brooded unseen, sunbeams playfully glinting off their bone china teaware. Yet come the strike of ten, as all will soon become enshrouded in obscurity, fortunes plummeted into a maelstrom of desolation.

The Hawthornes' refuge would descend into chaos — dread curdled into tortured cries as the wicked scheme would unfurl. With their world which shadows would besiege, and a stark melancholy beset their once-enchanting dwelling.

As their sanctuary would crumble amid evil snarls and the cacophony of misery, harmony surrendered to devastation. Another mournful story is unfolding to bear testimony: unto darkness, even the noblest dreams may fall — revealing true colours hidden beneath perfidious facades.

In the golden glow of morning, a sinister shadow lay heavy over the verdant lands of Queenstown, South Africa. The nefarious Edward Stokes and his merciless band of villains thundered upon the once tranquil homestead of Lord and Lady Hawthorne, intent on treachery and deceit. The skies whispered warnings as the nefarious band approached, a horde of twenty mounted marauders armed with deadly weapons and hearts devoid of humanity.

With ruthless abandon, they seized Lord Hawthorne from his sanctuary and whisked him away for unspeakable torments. Lady Hawthorne's helpless cries pierced the air as wicked hands forcibly detained her. Tender-hearted as she was, her spirit was shattered beneath the weight of her own grief and desolation. And there stood Edward Stokes, venom dripping from his words as he cruelly declared his intent — to seize the Hawthorne businesses for himself and enslave Lord Hawthorne within his iron bonds.

Thus Lady Hawthorne bore her helpless yoke, forced to play the part of a dutiful wife to an undeserving husband, lest her beloved Lord Hawthorne suffer even more disgraceful treatment. In this vile act of betrayal, Edward Stokes committed one final, unforgivable sin: invading the sacred sanctity of Lady Hawthorne's bedchamber to debase her honour till nothing sacred remained.

Locked away in Edward Stoke's Mountain lair called Blaauwater, Lord Hawthorne languished under watchful eyes that never ceased their relentless glare. The whereabouts of his dismal prison remained hidden far from those who might have sought him out. His heart ached for the fair wife torn so cruelly from his side.

Unspeakable shame burned in Lady Hawthorne's breast when she discovered she carried Edward Stoke's child, forged by his deceitful cruelty. And when their daughter Clare took her first breath in this cruel world, they circumvented her knowledge about the deceit that her birth shrouded.

Clare grew into a winsome lass, her delicate beauty reflective of Lady Hawthorne's tender heart. After the charade's continuation, they returned to their long-empty family manor in England. People whispered about their mysterious absence in hushed tones but remained unaware of Edward Stoke's monstrous deception.

Edward Stokes played puppet master with Lady Hawthorne's destiny, unwavering in his callous grip on her life even as he traversed between South Africa and England to oversee his undeserved empire. His ghastly vow to extinguish Lord Hawthorne's life should Lady Hawthorne break her silence echoed endlessly in her tormented heart.

Lord Hawthorne stood a broken man in the cavernous cell of Blaauwater's depths, nourished only by the fading memories of his former happiness and an unyielding desire for justice. Time drew on, and they danced to Edward Stoke's twisted tune — but hope lingered, for there are few things as resilient as a love forged through shared adversity. And sometimes, even the darkest lies are unearthed by the gentle touch of truth.

Rescue of Lord Hawthorne

In the shadowy corners of Victorian England, the villainous business manager, Edward Stokes, unfolded his treacherous plans with a sinister smile on his malicious face. The noble Lord Hawthorne found himself ensnared in a web of deceit and secrets, locked away in the dank cells of Blaauwater Estate, while his loving wife suffered the cruel torments of bondage at home.

Sworn to protect the innocent, Jacob, the valiant champion of justice, called upon his most trusted companions from England and South Africa. Assembled were men and women of extraordinary skill and courage, like a brotherhood infused with fierce determination and unmatched expertise.

Under the veil of night, they scoured for intelligence on Blaauwater's treacherous defences, keen eyes seeking every clue to penetrate its hostile walls. Methodically, their daring plan took shape as they plotted a course through moonlit shadows in hopes of outwitting their enemy.

Securing every weapon and supply necessary for this deadly assault, they armed themselves to face any challenge. Jacob's team sharpened their skills through rigorous training sessions that tested their physical limits and mental strength.

As planned, darkness enveloped Jacob's team as they approached Blaauwater from both sides; fear no obstacle in their mission to save Lord Hawthorne. Each heartbeat synchronised with hands firm on rifles and pistols that were ready at a moment's notice.

Sweat poured from their brows as they fought a desperate struggle against Edward's trained assassins.

Deadly combatants clashed ferociously in fierce hand-to-hand battles while other fighters fired from their deadly rifles and pistols' rapidly waning ammunition. Were it not for Jacob's elite team's grit and unwavering determination, the nefarious guards would have prevailed.

They carried the battered Lord Hawthorne into the darkness of freedom with a mighty surge. Shadows once again served as their cloak as they navigated a treacherous escape route from Blaauwater, keeping their precious cargo safe from harm.

In the end, the triumphant warriors reflected on their daring mission, their unity in alliance stronger than ever. Edward Stokes' treachery was met with the swift and unforgiving grip of justice, serving as a stark reminder that in the face of darkness, there will always be a valiant few ready to stand as defenders of light.

Lord Hawthorne had languished in the depths of a forgotten prison, enveloped by shadows and whispers of deceit. His soul yearned for the touch of the sun, his spirit haunted by visions of freedom that danced just beyond his reach. The cold walls held him captive, a prisoner to his own thoughts, shackled by the iron grip of despair.

The only solace he had found came in the form of tattered scraps of parchment and a humble pencil. Through them, he would bleed ink from his very soul, weaving words like silken threads that stretched forth into the abyss — letters of love penned to his beloved Eleanor, an ethereal muse who lived only in his dreams. Each stroke birthed hope, quivering with melancholy.

Yet those fragile letters were like phantoms that could never pierce through the veil surrounding him. Cut off from humanity, his heartfelt prose remained but whispers in the night, silently crying out for connection and compassion amid an ocean of desolation.

So there, Lord Hawthorne had stood still and stoic, his heart entwined with longing and betrayal. As days melded into nights, they became indistinguishable under the shroud of darkness, a never-ending symphony of yearning intertwined with treachery.

And in this haunting world where shadows skulked and time seemed to weep in slow motion, he had clung desperately to his paper-thin solace, fighting to keep alive the flicker of hope against the encroaching tide of deception and despair. He was now free!

My dearest Eleanor,

In the depths of my confinement, amidst the haunting shadows that dance upon my cell, my heart clings to the abiding love we share with fervent tenacity. Five arduous years have suffered in this forsaken corner of South Africa, but still, the memory of your tender embrace reignites an undying flame within me. I write my love for you when I can in my book of tattered pages.

I reminisce upon our autumn strolls through the amber woods, hand in hand, our love weaving an impenetrable bond — a safeguard from the terrors that dwell in this remote abyss. My captors bear down upon me with icy grasp, but they shall not extinguish my spirit, nor shall they sever the connection between us.

Eleanor, my beacon of light, each day brings me a renewed determination to escape this desolate prison to be reunited with you. I have devised ingenious plans and secret alliances; your unwavering love fuels my courage and resilience. The very thought of hearing your melodic voice once again hastens my pulse with unbridled anticipation.

Know this, my love — though we may be physically apart, our hearts remain entwined beyond time and distance constraints. We shall conquer this adversity together, our passion blinding even the cruellest tormentor's gaze.

My sweet Eleanor, keep our memories burning like a vigil in your soul until we stand united again. Suspend any doubts from creeping into your thoughts; for it is written within every fibre of my being that we will find each other again.

To you — my beloved wife – I pledge every shred of strength I possess. Your radiant image sustains me through these sombre nights in these torturous chains. Await me beyond the jagged horizon where our love remains everlasting.

In eternal devotion,

Thomas

My Dearest Eleanor,

In the darkest confines of this shanty prison, the brilliance of your love still finds a way to pierce through the bleakness that has enshrouded me. As I etch these words into the worn pages of this scrapbook, I hold onto the hope that one day they will reach your tender embrace.

My captors, unfathomably cruel and driven by avarice, do not understand our devotion. But their nefarious acts shall never extinguish our love's fire. Even while shackled, my heart roams free—with every beat navigating back to you.

Days morph into weeks and then into months, with time seemingly converging into perpetual dusk. Each moment that passes is but an affirmation of our indomitable love. It carries with it the beauty of a rose in full bloom but also bears the sharpness of its thorns; but my dear, it is the thorns that enable us to cherish its magnificence all the more. The pain serves as a harsh reminder—an enduring symbol—of all we have endured and have yet to overcome.

Oh, Eleanor, my sweetest confidante and treasured love, if only these pencilled confessions could reveal the depth of my emotion toward you. With your extraordinary grace and elegance, I am convinced that Providence itself held the quill as it penned our tale—a story containing passion's tribulations and triumphs beyond anything my battered mind could describe.

As we remain apart by cruel circumstances, we know that nothing in this world can sever the bonds forged in our hearts. We shall vanquish this tormenting foe, for our transcendent love outshines their iniquitous darkness.

So do not believe for a second that our spirits are distant. My darling Eleanor—your memory fuels my soul and imbues me with strength in these harrowing times. Even when enveloped by darkness, a single spark of our love is enough to guide me home, where I hope we will soon be reunited.

Your devoted Thomas

Under the veil of a sanguine twilight, Lord Hawthorne's heart raced with the anticipation of reuniting with his beloved Eleanor. Still weak from his torment, an unwavering fire of devotion guided him forward with each step he took. Jacob, his gallant saviour, stood by his side as they journeyed through the arduous terrain — their unspoken bond thriving on a shared passion for their loved ones.

Meanwhile, Lady Hawthorne, tucked away in her secret refuge in the tantalising landscapes of South Africa, clung to hope like a fragile rose caught in a tempest. She yearned for the moment she would see her husband's face again and breathe him into every fibre of her being. Her name had become synonymous with resilience amidst uncertainty.

As they traversed the winding trails, Jacob revealed poignant secrets that lay hidden behind a tangled web of deception Edward Stokes had spun around them. Lord Hawthorne listened attentively, his mind painting images of Clare - a beacon of light amidst profound darkness. She seemed to resemble her mother in countless ways, embodying love and gentleness as if it were instinct rather than inheritance. His heart swelled for Jacob and Clare as their passionate tale unfolded before him.

When at last, they reached their beautiful reunion's precipice, a sea of emotions cascaded within Lord Hawthorne's weary body. Time had etched its mark upon him, but within dwelled a passion that transcended his limits. As he prepared to glimpse Eleanor after countless years apart, his heart burned like an eternal flame, and he knew joy beyond measure would soon be theirs to share.

Moments coalesced into eternity as Lord Hawthorne whispered Eleanor's name onto the waiting wind; anticipation clung to every beat of his pulse — ready and yearning for their hearts to collide once more, intertwined as destined lovers.

At long last, the monumental moment had arrived, a pivotal juncture that would forever alter their fates. Around the enigmatic bend lay Eleanor's clandestine sanctuary — a hallowed refuge soon to be transformed into a bastion of hope for Lord and Lady Hawthorne. The veil of anticipation was about to be lifted as he stood on the precipice of reuniting with his cherished beloved.

Outside, Lady Hawthorne roamed restlessly, her movements akin to a fierce lioness yearning to claim its quarry. A torrent of emotions surged within her as her heart danced to a frenetic beat. An avalanche of thoughts cascaded through her mind, muddying the waters of what she would say and do upon beholding her cherished other half.

And then it came — the dishevelled carriage bearing Lord Hawthorne arrived in a whirlwind of fervour. Imbued with a steely resolve forged from relentless desire and interminable waiting, he emerged unwaveringly from his chariot, unburdened by any need for assistance. There she was: sweet Eleanor, weeping crystalline cascades of euphoria, her very being quaking at the sight of her noble knight. As if drawn by an unseen force, Eleanor sprinted towards Lord Hawthorne; reciprocating this magnetic pull, he extended his arms with every ounce of fortitude remaining and enfolded his precious Eleanor into a loving embrace, enmeshing their souls into one.

As they clung tightly to one another, their hearts threatened to shatter the cage of their ribs — neither dared entertain the notion that they might ever be torn asunder again lest this wondrous vision might disappear like the morning mist. They raised their tear-streaked visages and gazed upon each other with an intensity that rendered all else insignificant. In this transcendent instant — this celestial fusion brimming with unbridled affection and joy – Eleanor and Thomas were finally reunited, now and forevermore.

Epilogue

It is over a year since the daring rescue of Lord Hawthorne, and serenity has draped itself over the lives of those once entangled in a tempest of danger. Lord and Lady Hawthorne have embraced semi-retirement as if kissed by destiny, finding solace in each other's arms while the Lord's health blossoms once more.

Jacob and Clare, their love entwined tighter than ivy on an ancient oak, eagerly await the arrival of their second child. Meanwhile, little Sarah plays innocently by the fire, her laughter as warm and sweet as the hot chocolate cradling in their hands while they nestle together in their new London home.

Outside, however, lies deception. The night air is heavy with an unyielding fog, shrouding secrets untold. Beneath this veil, darkness creeps across worn cobblestones in sharp contrast to the loving embrace within.

Suddenly, a knock disrupts the comfort of their intimate abode. Jacob's heart leaps into his throat as he rises to investigate. Opening the door cautiously, he discovers a woman huddled on the steps – Nan, the gypsy lady whose friendship had blossomed in Ireland and now his business accomplice. Her face a canvas of pain and mystery — blood, evidence of misfortune — painting her forehead and hands.

As if carried by a ghostly wind, she whispers cryptic words that steal Jacob's breath away. Her frail body succumbs to unconsciousness.

Clare meets Jacob near the front door, anxious concern rising like smoke from glowing embers. Her voice quivers with apprehension, "Is this Nan? What is wrong?"

A tumultuous storm of anxiety brews within the depths of Jacob's gaze, his eyes reflecting an unyielding turbulence. His voice, trembling with desolation, intertwines with the weight of helplessness, reminiscent of gnarled vines ensnaring a time-worn ancient bridge embedded in forgotten realms. Gasping for breath, he utters with utmost urgency, "Nan; she desperately requires our aid, and in this dire moment, our very lives teeter on the cusp of peril..."

And so begins a tale of danger intertwined with desire as fierce as dragon's breath; each chapter daring and inspiring action — plunging our dear protagonists into uncertain waters where love and suspense linger like shadows on a moonlit night.

Beneath the beguiling glow of a silvery moon, shadows stir to life, weaving a tale of clandestine desire and heart-pounding suspense. Embark on a thrilling journey with Jacob, Clare, and their intrepid circle of friends as they uncover secrets wrapped in whispers and deceit, plunging headlong into a world of action, daring, and inspiration.

Don't miss this pulse-quickening episode; secure your place in a world where romance merges with peril at every turn. Register now to ensure you won't miss a single heartbeat as this extraordinary saga unfolds before your eyes.

Shadows on a Moonlite Night by KJ Winchester

Don't miss out!

Visit the website below and you can sign up to receive emails whenever KJ Winchester publishes a new book. There's no charge and no obligation.

https://books2read.com/r/B-A-VCKY-AIAJC

BOOKS 2 READ

Connecting independent readers to independent writers.

Also by KJ Winchester

Entangled Hearts

Watch for more at www.theblogletters.com.

About the Author

In a world where shadows dance, and secrets whisper, KJ Winchester weaves spellbinding tales of romantic thrillers, mystery, and intrigue that ignite the imagination. Winchester masterfully layers love and danger in each short story, creating an intoxicating blend that will inspire the heart and quicken the senses.

Enveloped in a shroud of mystique, Winchester's characters come to life amidst complex plots and breathless twists. Their passions simmer beneath the surface, waiting to be unleashed at the most unexpected moments. As the tension builds to its crescendo, readers find themselves irresistibly drawn into a realm of intrigue and seduction - where love conquers all and inspiration blooms in even the darkest corners.

Embark on a journey with KJ Winchester, where mystery intertwines with inspiration, leaving you breathless for more. In this realm of romantic thrillers, prepare to delve into a world that captivates and enthrals with every word, turning every page into an adventure you'll never forget.

Read more at www.theblogletters.com.